# the CRiTTeR club

## :: Marion and the Secret Letter ::

by Callie Barkley ♥ illustrated by Tracy Bishop

LITTLE SIMON

New York  London  Toronto  Sydney  New Delhi

LITTLE SIMON

An imprint of Simon & Schuster Children's Publishing Division · 1230 Avenue of the Americas, New York, New York 10020 · First Little Simon hardcover edition February 2017 · Copyright © 2017 by Simon & Schuster, Inc. All rights reserved, including the right of reproduction in whole or in part in any form. LITTLE SIMON is a registered trademark of Simon & Schuster, Inc., and associated colophon is a trademark of Simon & Schuster, Inc. For information about special discounts for bulk purchases, please contact Simon & Schuster Special Sales at 1-866-506-1949 or business@simonandschuster.com. The Simon & Schuster Speakers Bureau can bring authors to your live event. For more information or to book an event contact the Simon & Schuster Speakers Bureau at 1-866-248-3049 or visit our website at www.simonspeakers.com. Designed by Laura Roode. The text of this book was set in ITC Stone Informal Std.

Manufactured in the United States of America 0117 FFG

10 9 8 7 6 5 4 3 2 1

Cataloging-in-Publication Data is available from the Library of Congress.

ISBN 978-1-4814-8703-0 (hc)

ISBN 978-1-4814-8702-3 (pbk)

ISBN 978-1-4814-8704-4 (eBook)

# Table of Contents

# A Secret Surprise

Marion, Ellie, Amy, and Liz stood watching their guest Dalmatian at The Critter Club. The dog hadn't eaten all day. She just stood by her full food bowl, not interested.

Marion went to a filing cabinet. She pulled open the drawer labeled *Critter Files*. She flipped through the files inside. There was one for every animal the girls had taken care of—ever since they'd opened the rescue shelter in Ms. Sullivan's barn.

Marion flipped past files for Digit the turtle, Lulu the French bulldog, Ollie the kitten . . . Marion smiled at the sight of Ollie's name. He was the kitten her family had adopted!

"Penny!" Marion called out, finding the file she needed.

Earlier that day, Penny's owner had dropped her off. She was going away for a week, so the girls had agreed to pet sit.

The last time Penny was at The Critter Club, it was because Amy had found her as a stray in a park. But the girls hadn't seen her since they found her a home. It was so good to have her back.

If only she would eat!

Marion pulled a fact sheet out of the Penny file.

"Here!" said Marion. "Penny's favorite dog food is Blue Ribbon."

FACT SHEET

NAME: Penny

SPECIES / BREED: Dog / Dalmation

FAVORITE FOOD: Blue Ribbon brand dry food

OTHER INFO: Found as a stray in park in Orange Blossom. Likes to chase frisbees and play with Rufus. Knows commands "sit" and "stay."

"We have some of that in the storage closet!" cried Liz. She hurried off to get some. The girls changed the food in Penny's bowl, and she dug right in.

"Good thing you're so organized, Marion," Ellie said.

Marion smiled. The Critter Files *had* been her idea. She made sure they were kept up to date.

Problem solved. The girls watched Penny eat as they talked about the weekend.

Liz had worked on the set for a play at the youth theater. Ellie had gone to the beach with her brother, Toby, and their nana Gloria. And Marion and her horse Coco had taken first place in their jumping competition.

"Wow!" Amy cried. "Congratu-lations!" The girls gave Marion hugs and high fives.

"Thanks," said Marion. "Coco did all the hard work."

Then Marion looked at Amy. "What about you? How was your weekend?"

Amy shrugged. "Oh, fine," she said.

Marion, Liz, and Ellie were quiet, waiting for more. But Amy was quiet too.

"That's it?" said Ellie.

Amy nodded. "I helped out at the clinic." Amy's mom was a

veterinarian. "Nothing exciting happened," Amy added.

But Marion noticed a flush of pink on Amy's cheeks.

"Hold on," said Marion. "You're blushing." It was usually a sign that Amy was feeling shy or embarrassed—or hiding something!

Amy's cheeks blushed a little redder. "No, I'm not," she argued.

Ellie eyed Amy suspiciously. "What are you not telling us?" she said slyly.

"Okay," Amy said. "I do know some exciting news. But I *promised* I wouldn't ruin the surprise."

"Surprise?" Marion cried excitedly. "Surprise for whom?"

Amy shook her head. "I *really* can't say."

"Are we getting a new Critter Club guest?" Liz asked. "Is it a lemur? Oh, I hope it's a lemur."

"Did someone famous bring in their pet?" Ellie asked.

Amy took a deep breath. "I *think* I can tell you this," she said.

Marion, Ellie, and Liz leaned in closer to hear what Amy would say.

"You'll find out about it . . . ," said Amy, "in school tomorrow."

"Tomorrow?" Marion moaned.

How could she wait that long to find out?

# Chapter 2

# The New Classmate!

At school the next morning, Marion hurried to unpack her backpack. She figured that the sooner she got to her desk, the sooner she'd find out what the surprise was!

*I hope we find out first thing this morning!* Marion thought.

She left her library books in her locker out in the hallway. She brought her homework to Mrs. Sienna's desk. At her own desk, she got organized.

Then, finally, Marion looked around the room. Amy, Ellie, and Liz were already at their desks too.

They traded smiles and knowing looks.

"Okay, everyone," Mrs. Sienna said from her desk. "Before we have our morning meeting, I have a surprise for you."

Marion sat up straight. She tapped her pencil on her desk in excitement.

Mrs. Sienna went on. "First of all, we have a guest." She looked toward the classroom door. "Please, come in, Dr. Purvis."

Marion shot another look at Amy. Her mom was here? Amy

smiled at Marion and nodded.

Dr. Purvis came in, wheeling a cart with something on top. Marion craned her neck to see. She gasped. It looked like a pet cage. The right size for a gerbil, or a guinea pig, or—

"A hamster!" Liz cried out in the first row.

Yes! Now Marion could see a furry brown hamster running in the exercise wheel inside the cage.

"Awwwww," the class cooed.

"Class, this is Amy's mom, Dr. Purvis," Mrs. Sienna said. "She's a veterinarian."

Dr. Purvis gave a wave. Then she pointed at the hamster. "And let *me* introduce you to . . . your new class pet!"

The room erupted in cheers.

Marion noticed the hamster jump at the noise. He darted into a corner.

"I think we're scaring him," Marion said gently. Everyone quieted down.

Dr. Purvis told the class she had given the hamster a full checkup over the weekend.

*Aha!* thought Marion. *So that's how Amy had known about the big secret!*

"I'm happy to report that he is a very healthy little hamster," said Dr. Purvis.

"And it will be up to us to help keep him that way," said Mrs. Sienna. "Each day our pet is in the classroom, someone will be assigned as the Hamster Helper. Dr. Purvis is going to tell us how to take care of him."

Amy's mom went over the basics. Their hamster needed fresh water each day, plus one scoop of his special food pellets—no more, no less!

His cage had to be cleaned every few days.

"Don't worry," Mrs. Sienna told the class. "I'll handle that job."

Finally, Dr. Purvis showed them all how to safely hold a hamster. "Always use two hands," she said.

Then Dr. Purvis wished them good luck, and headed out the door. "Call me with any questions!" she said as she went.

"Thank you, Dr. Purvis!" Mrs. Sienna called. Turning to the class, Mrs. Sienna smiled. "Now, I think we'd better give this little guy a name!"

- BROWNIE
- BOB
- GUS
- HAMMY
- SUPERHAM
- SIR HAMSTER McSMARTYPANTS

Hands flew up all around the room. Mrs. Sienna called on students one by one. She wrote their name suggestions on the whiteboard.

Students laughed as the suggestions got sillier and sillier.

Then Marion raised her hand. Mrs. Sienna called on her. "He's so cute and cuddly. How about Teddy?"

"Awwwwww," the whole class said together.

Mrs. Sienna clapped. "I think we have a winner!" she said. "Teddy it is!"

# Chapter 3

# Marion Puzzles It Out

Marion waited her turn to go across the monkey bars.

Ellie had just gone. Amy was swinging her way across now. And Liz was up next.

It was recess. The girls were playing and talking about the events of the morning.

"I can't believe you were able to

keep it a secret!" Ellie said to Amy. "A class pet!"

Amy got across the last few rungs. "It was so hard not to tell you guys!" Amy admitted.

Liz started across the bars. "Teddy's pretty adorable," she said.

Marion agreed. "I really, really,

really hope Mrs. Sienna draws my name today!" she exclaimed.

Mrs. Sienna had saved the best news for last. Every Friday, she would draw a different student's name out of a bowl. That student got to take Teddy home for the weekend!

But today, this very afternoon,

someone would get to take him home for three days! Dr. Purvis had suggested that Teddy only spend one or two days in the noisy classroom during his first week.

Marion crossed the monkey bars, then dropped down to the ground. She glanced around the playground.

Some kids were playing touch foot-ball. Others were jumping rope. A few were swinging on the swings. Joey, a boy from Mrs. Sienna's class, was off by himself near the cafeteria door.

Marion looked again. Joey was walking slowly with his head down. He was looking around on the ground.

Curious, Marion jogged over.

"Did you lose

something?" she asked Joey.

Joey looked up. "Not exactly," he said with a smile. "I just can't *find* something."

Marion must have looked puzzled, because Joey laughed, then explained.

"I started a scavenger club," Joey said. "Michael, Jamil, and Abby are in it too." They were all second graders, except Michael, who was in third.

Joey unfolded a piece of paper he was clutching in one hand. "We take turns making up scavenger

hunts for one another. You start with one clue. If you can figure it out, it leads you to another clue. Then that one leads you to another and . . . you get the idea."

Joey showed Marion the clue.

Some flowers are red.
The sky is blue.

Can you find the note with the next clue?

"I can't figure this one out," Joey said. "I've been looking all around these red flowers." Joey pointed to some petunias growing next to the building. "But I can't find the next clue anywhere." Joey sighed.

Marion thought it over. *Red flowers . . . Blue sky . . .*

Suddenly, she had an idea. "Follow me!" she told Joey.

Marion ran over to the jungle gym. It had a ladder on one side, and two slides on the other side. A bridge connected the two sides.

Underneath the bridge was a play area. Marion ducked inside it.

"Look!" Marion pointed at some flower decorations on the jungle gym posts.

Joey gasped. "Red flowers!"

Marion looked up at the underside of the bridge. It was painted a light blue color. "And a blue sky!" Marion said.

Joey looked around on the ground. He spotted a folded piece of paper half buried in the wood

chips. He picked it up. Someone had written *Clue #2* on the outside.

"Wow, Marion!" cried Joey. "You're good at this! I never would have solved that one."

Marion beamed proudly. "Scavenger Club *does* seem like fun!" she said.

"Want to help me with this next clue?" Joey asked her.

Just then, the principal blew the

whistle. Recess was over. It was time to go back to class.

"Oh well," Marion said to Joey as they ran to line up. "Maybe another time!"

# chapter 4

# A Very Close Call

The school day dragged on. After recess, there was math, then library, then a science unit on plants. Marion was measuring a bean sprout growing out of a wet paper towel. But she kept forgetting the number before she wrote it down. All she could think of was the number of minutes until the end of the

day. That's when they'd find out who would take Teddy home!

Finally, at pack-up time, Mrs. Sienna picked up the bowl on her desk. "Remember," Mrs. Sienna said. "Everyone who wants a turn *will* get a turn to take Teddy home. But the *first* person to host Teddy at their house will be . . ."

Mrs. Sienna reached into the bowl of names. She mixed the pieces of paper with her hand. Then she pulled one out.

"Marion Ballard!"

Marion jumped out of her seat. She could not believe her luck!

"Congratulations, Marion," said Mrs. Sienna. She asked Marion to go out at pickup time to check with her mom or dad. "If it's okay with them, you can come back in to get Teddy and his things."

"Okay," Marion replied.

Right away, Marion started making a list in her head. It was a list of reasons why her mom just couldn't say no.

Whether it was Marion's reasons, or Teddy's cute little face, Mrs. Ballard had agreed. Teddy was their houseguest!

Marion had placed Teddy's

cage in her bedroom, on top of the dresser. She had washed and refilled Teddy's water bottle. But she was waiting to feed him his pellets until the morning.

Marion and her little sister, Gabby, sat on Marion's bed, keeping an eye on Teddy. It was so

much fun just to watch him scamper around his cage.

Teddy peeked out at them, his whiskers twitching.

"Can't we take him out?" Gabby asked Marion. "Can I hold him? Please, please, please?"

Marion nodded. "I guess so," she

said. "But we have to be careful. Okay?"

Gabby agreed. So Marion reached in and gently scooped Teddy up. "See how I'm holding him with two hands? Cup your hands just like I am."

Gabby cupped her hands, and Marion placed Teddy inside.

Gabby smiled a huge smile. "Hello there, Teddy," Gabby said in a sugary-sweet tone.

Keeping her hands wrapped around him gently, Gabby rubbed Teddy's fur with her thumb. "He's soooo soft," Gabby said.

She shifted one of her hands to pet the top of Teddy's head.

In a flash, Teddy wriggled out. He scurried away across the bedspread.

"Oh!" Gabby cried.

"Oh, no!" Marion exclaimed. "Teddy!"

Marion lunged across the bed after him. Teddy darted out of her reach. He ran all the way to the end of the bed. Then Teddy paused, peering over the side.

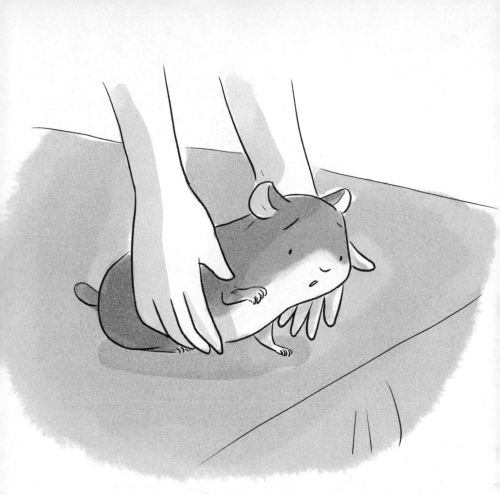

It was just enough time for Marion to catch up. She closed her hands gently around Teddy.

Marion quickly put him back into his cage, safe and sound.

Gabby wrapped her arms around Marion. "I'm sorry," Gabby said quietly. "I didn't mean to—"

"It wasn't your fault, Gabby," Marion interrupted. "Teddy's just super quick!"

It *wasn't* Gabby's fault, but still, Marion was really relieved.

What if she'd had to tell the class that Teddy had run away?

# Teddy's on a Roll

On Tuesday, Marion told her friends how Teddy had jumped out of Gabby's hands. Amy suggested getting him a hamster ball.

"You know," said Amy, "the hamster goes inside, starts running, and the ball rolls around. In one of those, Teddy could play outside his cage without getting lost."

"Good idea!" Marion cried.

So after school, Mr. Ballard drove Marion and Amy to Santa Vista Pet Supply.

The store was huge. There was a whole aisle for all the different dog

and cat foods. They had a reptile department with big glass tanks and heat lamps. They had a fish section with bags of aquarium gravel, swim-through castles, and water filters.

Marion and Amy quickly found the aisle for hamster, gerbils, and guinea pigs. There were exercise wheels, hideaways, tunnels, ladders, and other things to make a hamster home super fun.

Marion and Amy picked out a blue-tinted hamster ball for Teddy.

On their way to the checkout, they ducked into the dog aisle. Amy couldn't resist getting a hot dog chew toy for Penny. Then she picked up another. "I better get one for Rufus, too," Amy said with a smile.

On their way out of the store, they passed a bulletin board covered in flyers. A few with animal

photos on them caught Marion's eye.

Marion reached into her pocket and took out a tiny notebook. She carried it with her wherever she went.

Marion wrote down the information from each flyer. Names, breeds, phone numbers—everything.

"I'll write it all up in a neat list," Marion told Amy. "I'll make copies for you, Ellie, and Liz. Don't you think we could help find homes for these critters?"

Amy nodded. "That's why we call it The Critter Club!"

Back at Marion's house, the girls went upstairs to see Teddy.

"We got something for you!" Marion told him through the side of the cage.

They took Teddy out, and placed him gently inside the hamster ball. Then they closed the lid and put it down on the rug.

Teddy took a few steps. The ball inched forward. He started to run. The ball rolled across the floor.

Marion and Amy laughed as they watched him explore. They sat down at opposite ends of the rug. Teddy rolled himself back and forth between them.

"What do you think, Teddy?"
Amy asked him.

Marion answered for him. "I
think he likes it!"

# Hamster Hunt

"Good morning, Teddy!" Marion said, rolling out of bed the next day.

She went over to her dresser. She peered inside the cage.

"Where are you hiding, Teddy?" Marion said playfully. "In the tunnel again?"

But the tunnel was empty.

Marion peered at the cage from all sides.

"Teddy?" Marion said, growing worried. "Gabby!" she called to her sister in the next bedroom.

Gabby shuffled in, still in her pajamas. "What is it?" she asked Marion.

"Did you take Teddy?" Marion asked, starting to panic.

"No," Gabby replied. She looked confused. "Why?"

Marion froze. The side hatch of the cage was open.

"Oh no," Marion moaned. "Last

night, I put Teddy back into the cage this way. But I guess I didn't close the hatch!"

Marion looked at Gabby, her eyes wide in alarm as she realized what had happened. Now she *was* panicking.

"Teddy got out!" cried Marion. "He could be anywhere! We don't even know how long he's been out."

Before long, Marion's family had organized a search party. Marion's parents were searching downstairs. Gabby and Marion were upstairs.

The girls started in Marion's room. "Maybe he hasn't gone very far," Gabby suggested. She crawled under Marion's bed.

Marion moved her desk out from the wall. She peeked behind it.

Gabby checked behind books on Marion's bookshelf.

Marion looked inside her closet. There were so many places for a hamster to hide! She looked every-where, from the top shelf to the back of the shoe rack on the floor.

As she searched the floor, Marion thought of Joey, searching the school-yard on his scavenger hunt. *This is way less fun,* she decided.

They spent as long as they could searching. But no luck.

Marion's mom called up: "Girls, it's time to get ready for school!"

Tears were welling up in Marion's eyes. How could she go to school? It was her job to look after Teddy, but she didn't even know where he was. Or if he was okay!

Mrs. Ballard came up the stairs
and gave her a big hug. "Dad and I
will keep looking," she told Marion.
"Okay? Try not to worry. I'm sure
we'll find him."

At school Marion kept her eyes on the floor as she headed to her locker. She hoped no one asked her about Teddy. What would she say? All she wanted was to get through the day. Then she could go home and keep looking for him.

Marion opened her locker. A folded piece of paper fluttered out and landed at Marion's feet.

She picked it up. On the outside, it read:

Clue #1

79

# Chapter 7

# Two Mysterious Clues

All through morning work, Marion kept sneaking peeks at the note. She reached into her desk and pulled it out again.

Marion's head was spinning. This was so weird. Missing something? Did the person who left the note know where Teddy was?

And how did they even know

that Teddy was missing?

In any case, the clue was easy enough to figure out.

When it was time for morning recess, Marion told her friends she had to check on something. Then she headed straight for the swings.

As she got closer, her heart beat faster. Part of her was hoping that Teddy would crawl out from somewhere. But Marion knew it was a crazy thought.

Then she spotted something. On the ground, next to one of the posts of the swing set, was a bright patch

of white. Another note!

The outside was labeled *Clue #2.*

Did you find it? Not quite yet!
Check out a book about animals who
are not pets.

Lots of adventures and lots of fun.
Especially the very first one.

Marion looked around. A thought occurred to her. What if this person didn't know where Teddy was? Was someone sending her on a scavenger hunt for no reason?

*A book about animals,* Marion thought. *Wild animals, not pets. Animal adventures . . . ?*

Marion had it! The Adventures of Sophie Mouse! It was one of her favorite book series about a little mouse who lives in the forest.

Marion read the clue again. It said *"check out*

a book." Check out, like from the library?

She had to get to the school library!

*Could I go right now?* Marion wondered.

The teachers on playground duty were talking to one another. They probably wouldn't notice if Marion slipped inside.

But if they did, she might get in trouble.

Marion glanced over at Amy, Liz, and Ellie playing tag with some other kids. She wanted to ask them for help. But she didn't want to get them in trouble too.

So Marion waited for the right moment. Then she made her move. She slipped in through the cafeteria

door. She turned left and went down the quiet hallway.

At the first corner, Marion stopped. Like a spy, she peeked around to see if the coast was clear. There were no teachers in sight.

She was about to round the corner and continue on.

But just then, she heard a voice behind her.

"Marion Ballard?"

Slowly, Marion turned and looked up. Towering over her was Mrs. Young.

The principal.

# Chapter 8

# Unexpected Treasure

Mrs. Young stood there, her arms crossed in front of her. "Why aren't you at recess, Marion?" she asked.

Marion opened her mouth to answer. Her mind raced to find the right excuse.

But Marion couldn't come up with anything to say—except the truth.

"I . . . lost something," Marion replied.

Mrs. Young's face softened. "Oh, all right," she said cheerfully. "Well, you know where the Lost and Found is? By the library door?" Mrs. Young pointed the way. "Go check it and then head back outside. Okay?"

Marion nodded. She decided not to say she was *pretty*

*sure* Teddy wasn't in the Lost and Found.

Mrs. Young went off down the hall. Marion walked on to the library, and straight into the section with the chapter books.

Marion knew exactly where to look for The Adventures of Sophie Mouse books. She pulled out book number one, remembering the clue: *Lots of adventures, lots of fun, especially the very first one.*

Marion flipped through the book. There was a note in the middle! It was labeled *Clue #3*.

Go back to square one, your very first clue. What you are missing Is inside something blue!

Marion frowned. Square one?

On the playground, there were squares marked with a number one

for hopscotch. But that didn't seem to go with "your very first clue." Her first clue had been in her locker. . . .

*Oh! "Back to square one" means "back to the beginning"!* thought Marion. The scavenger hunt began at her locker.

And her locker was blue!

Marion's locker was right down the hall, back the way she'd come in. She practically ran there, wondering if there was any chance that Teddy was in her locker.

Marion unlatched the door and threw it open.

Teddy wasn't there.

Everything was just as she remembered it: notebooks, library books, her pencil case with a sticky note on it.

Wait. A sticky note?

Marion pulled it off and read it.

"Found it?" Marion said out loud. Found *what?*

And where was Teddy?

# Chapter 9

# The Principal's Office

Kids were streaming down the hall, back from recess.

Marion spotted Joey.

"What is this?" she asked him, holding up the sticky note. "What did I find?"

Joey smiled. "Your pencil case!" he replied.

Marion looked at him, confused.

"You left it on your desk yester-
day at dismissal time," said Joey. "I
tried to catch up to give it to you.
But you were gone. So I decided to
make a scavenger hunt for you!"

Marion's heart sank. This didn't
have *anything* to do with finding
Teddy.

"My pencil case?" Marion said
in disbelief. She hadn't even noticed
it was missing. *"That's* what I was
looking for all along?"

Joey seemed surprised by Marion's reaction. "Did I do something wrong?" he asked her. "You seemed interested in Scavenger Club."

Marion shook her head. "No, you didn't do anything wrong.

I'm just . . . worried about something else." She managed a smile. "Actually, that was a great hunt you put together. Thank you," she said sincerely.

But back at her desk in class, Marion moped. She looked down at her pencil case. It *was* nice of Joey to return it. But she would have traded it for Teddy in a second.

Just then, the classroom phone rang. Mrs. Sienna answered.

"Marion," she said after hanging up. "Mrs. Young would like you to see you in the main office."

Marion gulped and stood up slowly. She shuffled out of the classroom and down the hall.

*Uh-oh. Did the principal change her mind?* Marion wondered. *Am I in trouble for being inside during recess after all?*

Marion gasped. *Or does she know I lost Teddy?*

Marion pushed the main office door open. Mrs. Young was standing behind the front desk. She was talking to a woman sitting in a guest chair.

"Mom!" Marion cried.

"Marion!" said Mrs. Young. "Your mom needs a quick word with you. I'll be in the back at my desk."

Mrs. Young left Marion and her mom alone in the reception area.

"What are you doing here?" Marion asked.

Her mom smiled. "I had to come talk to you," Mrs. Ballard said. "I know you were worried this morning. About Teddy."

Marion was confused. "I'm *still* worried about Teddy," she said. "He's lost."

Mrs. Ballard shook her head. "Not anymore! We found him!"

"You did?!" Marion shouted. She was startled by how loudly that came out.

"Where was he?" she asked more quietly.

Marion's mom laughed. "Your dad went to put on his shoe this morning. And there was Teddy, nestled inside. A furry surprise!"

Marion sighed a huge sigh. She wrapped her arms around her mom and squeezed her tight. She had never felt so relieved in all her life.

Marion's day had just gone from a zero to a ten.

# chapter 10

# Teddy's Return

The next day, toward the end of school, Marion watched the clock.

The class was starting to pack up. *They have no idea,* thought Marion. *They're going to get an end-of-the-day surprise!*

Sure enough, at exactly 3:14, there was a knock on the classroom door.

Mrs. Sienna opened the door. "Well, hello, Mrs. Ballard!" she said, greeting their visitor.

Marion's mom walked in, carrying Teddy in his cage. All the kids

Teddy

Hamster

gathered around excitedly to peek in and say hello.

"And hello to you, too, Teddy!" Mrs. Sienna added.

The class gathered around the

little hamster, so excited to see him again.

Then Mrs. Sienna reached into the bowl of names. She pulled one out. "Joey!" she announced. "Congratulations! You are Teddy's next host!"

"Yes!" Joey yelled in excitement.

Marion's mom had brought all of Teddy's things: his food, his water bottle, and the new hamster ball. Marion showed it to Joey and advised him to use it. "Otherwise

Teddy can get away from you pretty fast," she said.

Joey gave her a thumbs-up. "Thanks for the tip!"

When the dismissal bell rang, Amy, Ellie, and Liz walked out with Marion and her mom.

"Are you going to miss Teddy?"
Ellie asked.

Marion nodded. "Yes," she said.
"I will." She looked at her mom and
smiled. "But Teddy *was* kind of a
handful."

Marion told her friends that she

had a *long* story to share.

"Maybe we can meet up at The Critter Club this afternoon," Liz suggested. "You can tell us all about it."

"Great idea!" said Amy. "I have something for Penny and Rufus."

"Oh! And *I* have a list!" said Marion, remembering her tiny notebook. She took it out of her pocket. It contained all the details from the pet supply store bulletin board.

Marion held it up to show her friends. "A list of some more animals who need our help!"

Read on for a sneak peek at the next Critter Club book:

#17

# Amy on Park Patrol

"Found another one!" Amy called out. She picked up an empty plastic bottle and put it in her recycling bag.

Amy was volunteering with Park Patrol, a group that cleaned up the Santa Vista Town Park. They met there one Saturday a month. Then they split up into teams to cover different areas.

Amy smiled proudly. She knew lots of wild animals lived in the park, like birds, squirrels, ground-hogs, and foxes.

"Okay. Thank you, Amy," said Mr. Schultz. "Next month we'll meet at the other end of the park. There will be some construction starting at this end."

"Construction?" said Jonah.

Mr. Schultz nodded. "The town has decided to build some stores here."

This section of the park was kind of wild. It didn't have bike paths or playgrounds or picnic areas. But to Amy, that's what was beautiful about it.

Amy didn't know what to think about this news. Was it good . . . or bad?

# the CRiTTeR club

## Join the club!